Horrible Harry
and the Triple Revenge

Horrible Harry
and the
Triple Revenge

BY SUZY KLINE

Pictures by Frank Remkiewicz

SCHOLASTIC INC.
New York Toronto London Auckland Sydney
Mexico City New Delhi Hong Kong Buenos Aires

ISBN-13: 978-0-545-03417-3
ISBN-10: 0-545-03417-5

12 11 10 9 8 7 6 5 4 3 2 1   7 8 9 10 11 12/0

Printed in the U.S.A.   40

First Scholastic printing, October 2007

Set in New Century Schoolbook

Dedicated to the love of my life,
my best friend and husband,
Rufus Orville Kline.
Thank you for helping me with my
twentieth Horrible Harry book!

Special appreciation to . . .

Frank Remkiewicz, for his inspired art and delightful sense of humor

My editor, Catherine Frank, for her very helpful comments

Quaker Hill Elementary in Waterford, Connecticut, which has regular "Snack Attacks!"

North Boulevard School in Pompton Plains, New Jersey. Thank you for inviting me to your Pajama Day.

My daughter, Emily Hurtuk, for telling me about the "Kitty-Litter Cake" created by Kellie Head, editor of ParentingHumor.com, from which Harry's birthday cake was adapted

And the original Milk Farm in Davis, California, which was the best place for ice cream between San Francisco and Sacramento!

Contents

The Ball and the Bug

My name is Doug, and I'm in third grade. I write lots of stories about my best friend, Harry. He's the guy in Room 3B who loves horrible things, slimy things, and gross things! His last name even *sounds* spooky—it's Spooger.

Harry is also the guy who loves Song Lee and gets bugged by Sidney.

But when something terrible happens at Southeast School, Harry always manages to make things better. Sometimes he even makes them fun! That's exactly what happened this week.

It all started on Tuesday before school.

Harry and I were just walking onto the playground. It seemed like a regular day. Mary was running up to everyone making sure they had done their homework.

"Harry," she said, "did you bring a wholesome snack like our teacher, Miss Mackle, asked?"

"I brought two," Harry bragged. "A healthy one and the one I plan to eat."

"Funny," Mary groaned, then she ran off to find Ida.

"Hey, Harry the Canary!" Sidney yelled from the ramp.

"Yo, Sid the Squid," Harry yelled back.

Sidney came running over to us. He had something in his arms. "You guys want to play with my brand-new soccer ball?"

"Sure," we said.

Harry smelled the new ball and flashed his white teeth. "It's leather!"

Sid beamed. "*Genuine* leather! I get to kick first!"

At that very moment, Song Lee joined us. She was holding something in her hand.

"I made this yesterday with my father," she said with a big smile.

Harry's eyes bulged. "A paper praying mantis! How cool is that!"

Song Lee giggled. "It's origami."

Sidney started tapping his foot. "Come on, you guys, we don't have that much time. Let's play ball!"

"Would you sit on it," Harry growled. "Just cool your jets!"

Sid sat on his soccer ball and steamed.

"How did you make that bug?" Harry asked Song Lee.

"The directions are in my origami book. The praying mantis is on page forty-nine. It's the most difficult one."

"Time is ticking away," Sidney groaned.

Harry ignored him. He was looking at page forty-nine. "Man, there are a hundred steps for making a praying mantis."

"It takes time," Song Lee said with a big smile. "And you need help."

"Does your bug stand up?" Harry asked.

"Yes," Song Lee said proudly.

We watched her set the praying mantis on the asphalt playground. The bug stood tall and didn't tip over.

Suddenly the bell rang.

Sidney jumped up and shouted, "Thanks a lot, El Tweeto!"

I couldn't believe what Sid did next. He stomped on the praying mantis, crushed it, and ran away with his soccer ball.

Song Lee immediately bent down and picked up the crumpled paper. She held it close to her heart. I saw her brush away a tear, then run over to line up.

Harry held up both fists.

"Double revenge?" I asked.

Harry shook his head. "Nope—*triple* revenge."

"Triple revenge?"

"It's the biggie," Harry explained. "And this time it means *three consequences* for Sidney La Fleur."

Oh boy, I thought, Sid was doomed!

Snack Attack!

When we lined up at the school door, Mary was the first to notice Song Lee. "Why are you crying?" she asked.

Song Lee shook her head. "It's . . . nothing," she whimpered. Then she wiped her eyes and didn't cry anymore.

Song Lee hardly ever tattled.

Mary looked back at us. We were the last ones in line. "I bet Harry did something," she growled.

Song Lee shook her head again. "No. I'm fine," she said.

Sidney was the first one to sit down in his seat and take out his writing notebook. He drew a soccer ball on a fresh page, then put it in a circle with a diagonal line. It looked like a "No Soccer" sign.

As the rest of us got out our notebooks, I wondered when Harry would get revenge number one. Right now Harry was just glaring at Sid across the aisle.

"Good morning, boys and girls," Miss Mackle said. "I hope everyone remembered their healthy snack. We're having a special visitor in a few minutes, and we want to be prepared!"

Harry reached into his backpack and pulled out two snacks. Both were

wrapped in foil. One was round. One
was square.

Just as he was putting both in his
desk, Sid leaned over and whispered,
"Can I have one? I forgot my homework.
I don't want anyone to know."

What nerve! I thought. El Creepo
was asking for a favor!

"Sure," Harry said, grinning. "I'd be
glad to share."

My eyes bulged. Harry was secretly
handing Sid the square snack. What
was Harry up to?

"Thanks, pal!" Sid said.

"Don't open it until you eat it," Harry added. "Keep it fresh."

"Gotcha!" Sid replied.

I just shook my head.

Miss Mackle went to the door. "I hear someone coming!"

We all looked up and heard singing in the hallway.

"YUM! YUM!

HERE I COME! COME!"

When it appeared in the doorway, Sidney yelled, "*Yikes!* It's a giant apple."

Dexter started singing to the tune of an Elvis song. "It ain't nothin' but an apple, walking in our room! It ain't nothin' but an apple, walkin' in our room!"

"SNACK ATTACK!" the apple boomed.

When our class went pin-quiet, ZuZu blurted out, "Who are you?"

"Apple Man," the creature boomed. "I'm looking for healthy snacks. I'm giving one point for each wholesome food. The class that has the best percentage of healthy snacks wins an extra recess."

Everyone cheered and clapped.

Except Song Lee. She was just quiet.

And Harry. He was looking at Apple Man's feet. "Those are Mr. Cardini's shoes," he whispered to me.

I looked down and nodded. It was our principal, all right. He was the big apple!

"Show me your healthy snacks," Apple Man demanded as he walked up and down the aisles.

"I have a banana," Ida said.

"I have yogurt," ZuZu said.

"Yum! Yum!" Apple Man replied.

"See my box of raisins?" Mary asked.

Dexter held up a carrot.

Song Lee had kiwi slices.

I had celery and green peppers.

"Deeeeeelicious!" Apple Man said. "I love vegetables and fruit!"

Apple Man added tally marks on his clipboard for Room 3B.

When he came to Harry, everyone held their breath. Harry slowly unwrapped his snack.

"Orange wedges," Harry said. "Grandma Spooger even left the white strings on them for me. I love pulp."

"YUM! YUM!

IN THE TUM TUM!"

Apple Man boomed.

Finally, Apple Man came to Sidney's

desk. He waited patiently while Sid unwrapped the four sides of foil. "I've got a healthy snack right here," Sid predicted.

Everyone watched him unfold the silvery paper.

Suddenly the smell of chocolate filled Room 3B.

"Fudge!" Apple Man said. "No points. NO CANDY FOR SNACKS!"

Sidney sank down in his chair.

Everyone groaned, "Sidney!"

Harry made a toothy smile. And when no one was looking, he put out his hand. "I'll take it back now, Sid the Squid!"

So that's what Harry was up to!

Revenge number one!

Sid made a face as he plopped the snack back in Harry's hand.

An hour later, Apple Man made an announcement over the intercom. "The winner of the Snack Attack today was Mr. Moulder's second-grade class. They had one hundred percent healthy snacks, so they get an extra recess!"

Room 3B groaned and moaned.

"We lost because of Sidney," Mary grumbled.

We all had long faces except for Harry. He was smiling as he held up two fingers.

Sid had *two more revenges* coming.

The Underwear Dare

Pajama Day was the big topic at lunchtime in the cafeteria. It was part of Spirit Week for Southeast School. Everybody was talking about it. Most of us had hot lunch that day. It was spaghetti and buttery garlic bread. The carrot sticks were good too.

As we slurped the noodles and crunched the bread and carrots, we talked about the big event.

"What are you wearing, Song Lee?" Ida asked. "I haven't decided what to wear yet. My pajamas or nightgown?"

Song Lee shrugged.

"I bet she brings her oragummy book," Sid said.

"Origami," Mary corrected.

When Song Lee didn't light up, Sid's smile disappeared. He could see she was still upset.

"We're having hot cocoa with mini marshmallows on Pajama Day," ZuZu said. "My mom is one of the room mothers. I know!"

"We get to read books anywhere in the room for a whole hour!" I said. "I'm reading the entire book of *Stone Fox*!"

"I'm bringing my own copy of *Revenge of Wedgie Woman*," Harry said, making his eyebrows go up and down.

After Mary cringed, she told us what she was wearing. "I have pink cat pajamas and pink fluffy slippers to match, and I'm bringing a book about Pinky and Rex. What about you, Doug?" Mary asked.

"I'm wearing a bathrobe," I said.

"Cool!" ZuZu replied. "What are you wearing, Harry?"

"Well, Zu, I don't wear pajamas to bed. I just go to sleep in my underwear."

Mary and Ida giggled.

"Hey, Harry the Canary," Sid said, "I've got a dare for you! Wear your underwear to school tomorrow for Pajama Day. It's what you wear to bed!"

Harry suddenly leaned way back in his lunch chair. He raised his bushy eyebrows, then pointed his carrot stick at Sidney. "Okay. Maybe . . . I will."

We all stared at Harry.

"You *will*?" Sid said.

"Maybe. On one condition."

"What's that?" Sid asked.

"If . . . I wear my underwear to school tomorrow," Harry replied, "you have to leap around all day like a praying mantis."

"Huh?" Sid said.

Harry gave a demonstration. He walked on his tiptoes with his head held

high. He moved his head from side to side. His hands were close to his chest, and his fingers wiggled back and forth.

Song Lee looked up. Thinking about a praying mantis made her eyes get watery. But Sid didn't even notice.

"It's a deal!" he said, looking at Harry. "You'll never wear your underwear to school!"

Harry shook Sid's hand. "We'll see about that."

Mary and Ida gasped, then covered their mouths.

Song Lee looked away.

I could only shudder. Harry's second revenge was risky!

The next morning was Wednesday. The bell was about to ring. Miss Mackle was at the bulletin board. Her hair was up in curlers, and she was wearing a granny nightgown.

Sidney was anxiously waiting by the door in his bright red pajamas with white snowmen. They were one size too big.

"Where's Harry?" Sid asked.

"Grandma Spooger always brings him to school on Wednesdays," I said. "That's when he has breakfast with his grandpa at Shady Glen."

Sid looked worried. "Do you think Harry's going to show up in his underwear?"

Ida shook her head. "I hope not. Cross your fingers that he doesn't."

Everyone crossed their fingers.

Except for Song Lee. She was reading a book called *A Single Shard* at her desk. She was wearing a pale blue nightgown with black-and-white pandas on it.

The rest of us waited at the door.

Finally, Harry strolled in.

Pajama Day

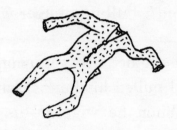

Harry was wearing underwear, all right.

Long johns!

Plain-white one-hundred-percent-cotton long johns!

I let out a big sigh of relief.

So did Mary and Ida.

Harry's teeth were as white as his winter underwear. "Okay, Sid. Start leaping like a praying mantis."

Sidney slapped the wall. "You tricked me!"

"So what were you expecting me to wear, Sid? Pull-up diapers?" Harry joked.

Sidney reluctantly got up on his tiptoes and pulled his hands close to his chest. When he wiggled his fingers, some of us giggled. He leaped very quickly over to his desk, holding his head up high like a praying mantis.

Ida and Mary giggled.

Sidney only got out of his seat four times that day.

Once to go to the bathroom.

Once to line up for lunch.

Once for dismissal.

And once to go to the refreshment table for hot cocoa and cookies. ZuZu's mom was handing out the treats. She noticed Sidney's funny steps. "Are you pretending to be an animal?" Mrs. Hadad asked.

Sidney half-smiled. "Actually, I'm pretending to be an insect," he mumbled.

ZuZu's mother looked at the teacher.

"I think Sidney has a good case of cabin fever," Miss Mackle chuckled. "That's why the school has Spirit Week in the middle of winter."

Mrs. Hadad smiled. "Well, Sidney, since you are an insect, you will like these Lebanese cookies. They have honey in them."

Sidney dropped a handful of marshmallows in his cocoa. "I will, thank you," he replied. Then he carefully leaped back to his desk.

Harry leaned back in his chair and flashed his white teeth.

His second revenge was done!

Now, I wondered, how far would Harry go for the third one?

The Third Revenge!

The next morning, when we lined up to go into the school, Harry announced his news.

"Guess what? I'm going to be nine on February sixth! Grandma is giving me a birthday party."

"No kidding?" I said. "That's so cool. What are you going to do?"

"It's a surprise," Harry said. "Grandma is taking us all to a special place in her Goog Mobile."

"*Goog Mobile?*" Mary and Ida shouted.

"It's a van named after his cat, The Goog," I explained.

"What's it look like?" Mary asked.

"Does it have whiskers?" Ida added.

"When you ride in it, you'll see," Harry replied.

"It's awesome!" I said. "I've seen it before in Harry's garage."

ZuZu and Dexter joined our conversation. Sidney looked on a few steps away.

"I've got the invitations with me today," Harry said in a low voice. He patted his back pocket. It was bulging. "I'm passing them out now before school. Read them after school, and don't talk about them. You know Miss Mackle says no handing out party invita-

30

tions in the classroom. It's rude. This is yours, Doug."

"Thanks," I said. "I like the cow sticker on the front." Then I put it in my pocket.

"Moo," Harry replied with a grin.

"This is yours, Song Lee," Harry said.

She tucked the invitation inside her flowered purse. Song Lee never talked about going to a party in front of other

people who weren't going. She wouldn't want someone to feel bad about not being invited.

Mary and Ida waited for their invitations. They smiled when Harry handed them each one.

"I can't wait to go to Harry's party," Mary said. "I know it will be different! Look! Even the envelope is different. It has a silly cow sticker!"

"Moo!" Ida giggled. "I love cows!"

Sidney stepped forward with his hand out.

Harry reached behind him. "This is yours, ZuZu. And yours, Dexter."

When the bell rang, we started to walk into the building. Sidney lagged behind with Harry and me. "You didn't give me mine."

"No, I didn't," Harry said.

Sidney paused, then dropped his head.

"Now you know how it feels to be crushed," Harry said. "Like Song Lee's praying mantis."

Sidney locked eyes with Harry. "I'm sorry I stepped on that oragummy bug!"

"You need to say that to someone else, Sid!" Harry snapped. "Not me!"

Sidney walked into the classroom with his shoulders humped over.

Harry's third revenge was the worst!

Sidney didn't get an invitation to the party.

Later that morning, during writing, I noticed Sidney was folding some green construction paper.

Harry was drawing a picture of Apple Man to go with his story, "The Adventures of Apple Man."

Song Lee was writing a poem.

I was writing about Pajama Day.

Suddenly Sidney walked over to Song Lee and handed her the crumpled-up green paper.

Harry and I looked up and listened to his conversation with Song Lee.

"This is for you," Sidney said. "I never realized how hard it was to fold paper to make a praying mantis. I'm really sorry I stepped on your oragummy. It was a rotten thing to do."

Song Lee held the green folded paper in the palms of her hands. It didn't look like a praying mantis. It looked like a big blob.

"It's okay," Song Lee said. "I can make another one. I feel better now."

"Do you forgive me?"

"Of course," Song Lee said with a warm smile. "Friends forgive each

other when they say they're sorry. I can tell you really mean it."

Sidney quickly wiped his eyes and went back to his seat. When he got there, he took out a Kleenex from his desk and blew his nose.

Harry got up to sharpen his pencil.

On his way back to his seat, he pulled out a white envelope from his back pocket and dropped it on Sidney's desk.

Sidney smiled when he saw what was on the front: a cow sticker!

It was an invitation to Harry's birthday party!

"Moo!" Sidney blurted out, then he quickly covered his mouth. When Miss Mackle looked over, Sid quickly apologized. "Sorry!"

Sid tucked the invitation away in

his backpack. He remembered Harry's instructions.

As soon as Harry sat down, I leaned over and whispered, "You had Sid's invitation all along?"

Harry nodded.

"You were planning to give it to Sid?" I asked.

"Yup, but not until three o'clock." Harry grinned. "I wanted him to suffer a little bit. But . . . I changed my mind."

I nodded.

I knew why.

Cow-Patty Party

You're invited!

Harry's ninth-birthday invitation was weird. It was brown and round.

And it was gross.

It was a cow patty.

There was a half-written poem inside that said:

Use your noodle.
Think of a barn.
We're going to party
At the _ _ _ _   _ _ _ _ !

What rhymes with 'barn'? I thought. Beats me!

I couldn't wait for the Goog Mobile to pick me up that Saturday at two o'clock. When I saw the big Volkswagen van turn the corner, I knew it was the Goog Mobile. There were flowers painted all over it, and on the side there was a big picture of Harry's cat.

Honk! Honk!

I waved good-bye to my mom, then ran out to the van.

Everyone else was inside, even Grandpa Spooger. His wheelchair was in the back. He and Harry's grandma sat in the front. Seven kids were strapped into the three rows of seats in the van.

"Hi, you guys!" I said, sitting next to Harry in the second row.

"This van is so cool!" Dexter said. "How old is it, Grandma Spooger?"

"I had it during my college days at Berkeley," she said. "During the sixties."

"Wow!" ZuZu said. "That means this Goog Mobile is about forty years old!"

"We take good care of it," Grandma Spooger said.

I noticed everyone had a present on their lap for Harry except Sidney. His was on the floor. He said it was too heavy to lift.

"Where are we going?" Mary asked.

"I gave you two clues on the invitation," Harry said. "The cow sticker and my poem. What rhymes with 'barn'?"

"There aren't too many words that rhyme with 'barn,'" Mary grumbled.

"Darn!" ZuZu replied. Then he laughed.

Grandpa Spooger laughed, too. "L-looks l-like you f-f-fooled them, H-Harry!"

"I did, Grandpa. But they even had a third clue. That invitation was one big cow patty. Where do you find those things?"

"I p-put one in m-my d-d-dad's mailbox once," Grandpa Spooger said. "We u-used to l-l-live on a f-farm in Indiana."

Song Lee giggled the loudest.

As the Goog Mobile passed grazing cows in the countryside, Mary called out, "I know. We're going to a farm!"

"All right!" Harry exclaimed. "You finally got it! The Milk Farm!"

ZuZu got out his invitation and read the poem with the two missing words:

Use your noodle.
Think of a barn.
We're going to party
At the M i l k   F a r m!

Mary made a face. "Harry Spooger! 'Farm' and 'barn' do not rhyme!"

"They almost do," Song Lee said. "It's still a fun poem."

Harry flashed Song Lee a toothy smile. "Dibs on sitting next to you at the party," he said.

Song Lee's face turned rosy red.

"Dibs on sitting next to the birthday boy!" Sidney added.

Harry rolled his eyeballs, but he didn't object.

It was exciting when we finally arrived at the Milk Farm! A huge wooden cow stood on the roof holding a gigantic strawberry ice-cream cone.

"Okay, everyone out," Grandma Spooger said. "Stay together now. We have a table reserved inside."

Everyone took their present with them to the Milk Farm. ZuZu and Dexter helped Sidney carry his. "Why is this so heavy?" ZuZu asked.

"You'll see," Sid said.

Grandma Spooger helped Grandpa Spooger into his wheelchair.

"L-let's e-eat!" Grandpa Spooger said.

Harry pushed his grandfather in his wheelchair carefully to the barn. I held the door as they went inside.

Grandma Spooger went back to the van for the cake. It was in one of her *A-1 Cakes* boxes.

"There's an ice-cream smorgasbord up there. Go help yourself, kids. Make yourself a super sundae," she said.

We all got in line and made our creations. Sid's had the most stuff on it. Song Lee put nine strawberries on her sundae. I made a banana split. When

Mary just ordered a Kiddy Cone, Harry said, "That's what I'm bringing home for The Goog." Mary just rolled her eyes as she licked her cone.

Harry chuckled as he made two hot chocolate fudge sundaes with whipped cream and nuts. One for his grandpa and one for himself.

After we enjoyed the ice cream, Grandma Spooger took out the cake she had baked for Harry's birthday.

It was horrible!

But Harry loved it!

The cake was inside a new litter box. The frosting had vanilla cookie crumbs with green sprinkles. The top was dotted with little Tootsie Rolls. One was hanging over the pan.

"Eweeyeee!" five of us said as Grandma Spooger got out a new pooper-scooper for serving the cake.

Harry and Sidney and Song Lee loved it. They clapped their hands and giggled!

"I don't think I can eat Harry's birthday cake," Mary said.

"Me neither," Ida and Dexter said.

"Maybe we should open the presents first," Grandma Spooger suggested. "We can cut the cake and sing 'Happy Birthday' a little later."

Harry didn't object. He dived into all the presents. He loved each one. I gave him a copy of *Stone Fox*, my favorite book. It's about an exciting dogsled race.

Song Lee made him a collection of origami insects, and included the origami book. The one on top was a praying mantis.

"Be careful with that one," Sid said.

Song Lee beamed.

Mary gave him a pair of pajamas with cows on them. Ida gave him a set of rubbery reptiles and amphibians. Harry liked the red salamander best.

Dexter gave him an Elvis CD. And ZuZu gave him the board game Clue.

Everyone was curious about Sidney's gift. It took two people to set it on the table. Its shape was big and weird.

"What do you think it is?" ZuZu asked.

"I already know," Harry said. "I asked Sid for it Thursday after school."

"You did?" Mary said.

"Yup. His stepdad works at Stone Memorials next to the cemetery. I asked for a leftover piece."

Everyone leaned forward as Harry tore off the birthday paper.

"A small boulder?" I said.

"Yup. Mr. LaFleur engraved my name and age in the granite rock. I'm keeping it in my bedroom. I'm going to sit on it and think of cool things to do."

"Oooooh," we all ooohed as Harry lowered the small boulder to the floor and sat on top of it.

"So, what are you thinking about now?" ZuZu asked.

"My birthday wish." Then Harry jumped off the rock and stood tall. "Got it!"

And that's when Grandma Spooger lit the candles on the cake and we sang "Happy Birthday." Harry blew out all nine candles with one breath.

Everyone did take a piece of the kitty-litter cake, although Mary didn't finish hers. Only Harry, Sid, and Song Lee ate the Tootsie Rolls.

It's hard to believe a week that started out so terrible could end up to be such fun.

But that's what happens when

friends forgive each other. And that's
what life can be like with Harry in
Room 3B.

Harry
Spooger
Age 9

Harry's Horrible Birthday Cake Recipe

Kitty-Litter Cake

Ingredients:
- 2 marble cake mixes
- vanilla frosting
- 12 sugar cookies
- green sprinkles
- 12 small Tootsie Rolls (Midges)

Directions:
1. Bake both cake mixes together in one large pan. Since doubling may require more cooking time, test

with a toothpick. If it comes out clean, it's done.

2. Place cooled cake in a new, clean kitty-litter pan.
3. Frost with vanilla frosting.
4. Crush the sugar cookies with a rolling pin. Sprinkle the crumbs on top of the frosting.
5. Add the green sprinkles on top.
6. Heat Tootsie Rolls in the microwave until soft (about 15 seconds). Drape the Tootsie Rolls on top of the frosting with the cookie crumbs. Hang one over the edge of the pan.
7. Serve with a brand-new pooper scooper.

Lebanese Cookie Recipe

Ingredients:

1/3 cup cooking oil

1/2 cup butter, softened

1/3 cup sugar

1 tablespoon orange juice

1 teaspoon baking powder

1/2 teaspoon baking soda

2 cups all-purpose flour

3/4 cup sugar

1/3 cup honey

1/2 cup water

1/3 cup finely chopped walnuts

Directions:

1. Beat cooking oil into butter.
2. Beat in sugar.
3. Add orange juice, baking powder, and baking soda. Mix well.
4. Add flour, a little at a time, to make soft dough.
5. Shape dough into 2-inch ovals and place on an ungreased baking sheet.
6. Bake at 350 degrees for 20 to 25 minutes or until golden.
7. Cool cookies on a rack.
8. Meanwhile, in a saucepan, combine the sugar, honey, and water. Bring to a boil. Boil gently, uncovered, for 5 minutes.
9. Dip cooled cookies into the warm syrup.
10. Sprinkle immediately with nuts.
11. Dry on rack.